G

GEO

Nicola Smee

RGE Goes Swimming

ORCHARD

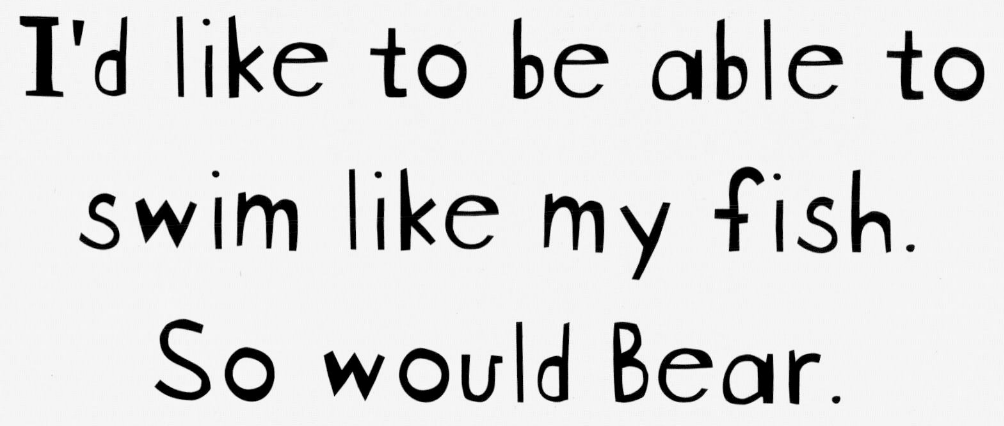

I'd like to be able to
swim like my fish.
So would Bear.

Mum takes us to the swimming pool.

Not the big pool, the little learner pool.

I'm ready!

But Bear is not.
He doesn't want
to get wet.

I'll go in
next time!

The water's lovely when you're in!

Come on, George!

Mum says I won't swallow the water if I keep my mouth closed . . .

Splutter!
Splutter!

. . . but it goes up my nose as well!

"Don't worry, you'll soon learn, George," says Mum.

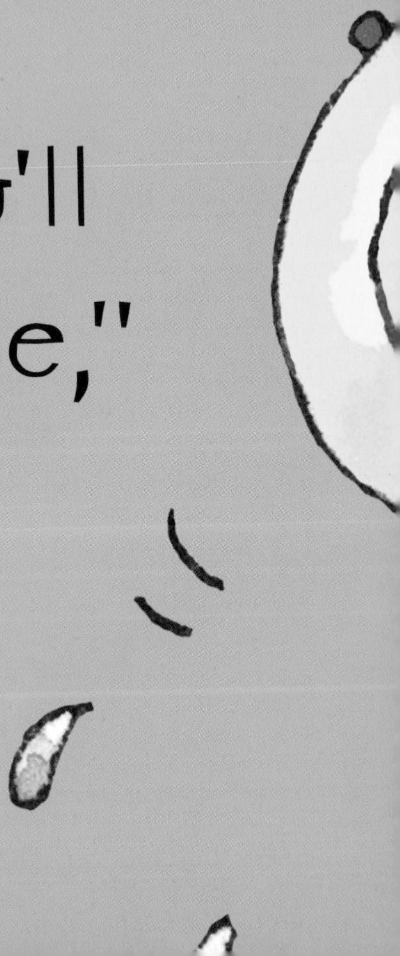

Sniff!

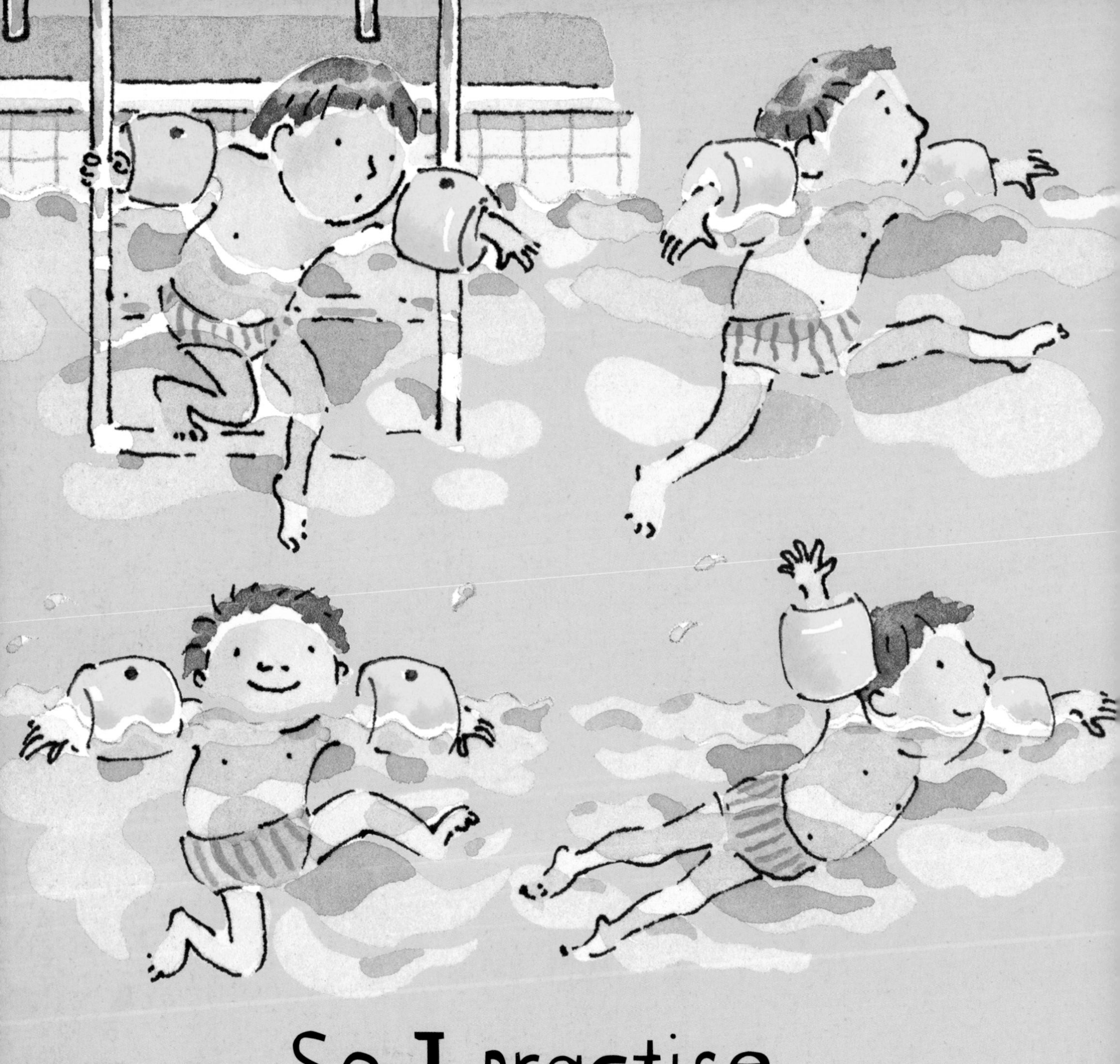

So I practise . . .

and practise.

Clap!
Clap!

Until at last . . .

I can swim just like my fish!

ORCHARD BOOKS
338 Euston Road, London, NW1 3BH
Orchard Books Australia
Level 17/207 Kent Street, Sydney, NSW 2000
First published in 1998 by Orchard Books
This edition published 2015 • ISBN 978 1 40833 557 4

A CIP catalogue record for this book is available from the British Library.
1 2 3 4 5 6 7 8 9 10 • Printed in China
Orchard Books is a division of Hachette Children's Books, an Hachette UK company.
www.hachette.co.uk